T0051324

To thine own SELF be TRUE

Hather

Thoughts

Ness

witty fool

MoRRoW

W

ABOVE ALL

A RoSE

merry

TIS TRUE

MY WORDS FLY UP

TO BE OR NOT TO BE

TO BRAVE

SH WIT

NEW

fog

Hither

COME

WORLD

WE CALL

THAT IS THE

Prologue

If by chance, young wordsmiths, you visit fair England, where we lay our scene, you will meet another collector of words named William Shakespeare.

Our tale begins when young William wakes to the morning light melting the darkness, whereupon he unlatches the window and hears the sounds of the busy street below. He listens to the call of the peddler, the clatter of a king's carriage, and the chatter of nearby neighbors. The world is waiting to be captured by his imagination.

Perchance this day of adventure will introduce new faces and inspire new words for William to write . . . if he can catch them.

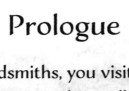

To bee, or not To bee

FLIBBERTIGIBBETY WORDS

Young Shakespeare Chases Inspiration

Donna Guthrie

illustrated by Åsa Gilland

PAGE
STREET
KIDS

One morning, William opened his window and words flew in.

PAPER, PENS, & PRETTY RIBBONS

MY WORDS FLY UP
MY THOUGHTS REMAIN BELOW
WORDS WITHOUT THOUGHTS
NEVER TO HEAVEN GO

The words dangled over William's head looking luscious and sweet. *I'd like to catch those words*, he thought.

William tried to scoop them up, but they were flibbertigibbety words that dipped and flipped and slipped through his fingers, glided downstairs, and leapt out the door.

BOLDNESS be my FRIEND!

Vaulting over the wall, the wayward words played hide-and-seek in his neighbor's garden.

"See how the words embrace my lady's roses and climb her balcony?" said the young gardener. "I will turn them into poems of love."

"These green-eyed words are jealous," said William. "They are not made for courtship."

WHAT'S IN A NAME? THAT WHICH WE CALL A ROSE BY ANY OTHER NAME WOULD SMELL AS SWEET

PARTING is such SWEET SORROW

CHAMBER POTS

The words caught a gust of summer breeze and drifted into the street. They turned handsprings over cobblestones and darted between pushcarts.

The king's three rose-cheeked daughters laughed as the words spun around their carriage wheels.

"I could use those strong words in my proclamations," said the old king.

"Those words are zany and madcap," said William. "They are too frivolous for proclamations. They came through my window, vaulted over a wall, and hitched a ride on the wheels of your carriage."

"And now they are off to the river!" the king cried.

The words skated along the slippery banks and into the water.

"I will use these adventurous words in my songs to lift the sails," said the sailor.

"They are useless words and not made for work," said William. "They came through my window, vaulted over a wall, took a turn on the old king's carriage, and now a storm might blow them out to sea."

A pair of fashionable twins stood nearby. "Try calling the words and make them come to you."

"Please good words," cried William. "Be well-behaved and come back!"

But the words skipped across the water.

BETTER a WITTY FOOL THAN a FOOLISH WIT.

William chased them across a bridge, past a farmhouse, through a graveyard, and into the majestic woods of Avon.

AND TURN HIS MERRY NOTE UNTO THE SWEET BIRD'S THROAT:

COME HITHER, COME HITHER, COME HITHER, COME HITHER.

The words danced onto the gnarled trunk of a greenwood tree and were captured in a robin's song.

William found the words simmering in a boiling pot stirred by three old women.

"These words bubble, bubble, and are too much trouble," said the women.

"Can I taste the words before I go?" said William. "They blew through my window, vaulted over a wall, took a turn on the old king's carriage, floated through the sailor's net, scrambled up a greenwood tree, were captured in a robin's song, and then dropped in your savory stew."

"These coldhearted words are not for a little schoolboy," said the women.
"They tell of gloomy castles and sad secrets. They belong in a tale of ours."
The women gave their brew another good stir and vanished into thin air,
taking the words with them.

William looked around the forest,
lonely and lost for words.

As William returned home disheartened, he met the town peddler.

"You look like a boy who could use a few kind words," the peddler said.

"I had words. They blew in my window this morning and led me on a wild goose chase. They vaulted over a wall, took a turn on the old king's carriage, floated through the sailor's net, scrambled up a greenwood tree, were captured in a robin's song, and simmered into a witch's brew. Then they vanished. What's done is done, the words are gone."

"Words will come again to a boy like you," said the peddler.

"Next time, capture the words with this." The generous peddler handed William a paper and pen.

That night, William opened his bedroom window and words flew in.

They were filled with memories of the eventful day and a hint of a story. They tumbled onto William's desk, telling of leaky ships and far-off lands, kings and witches, roses and love letters.

'TIS TRUE

O BRAVE NEW WORLD THAT HAS SUCH PEOPLE IN'T!

INK

PARTING IS SUCH SWEET SORROW, THAT I SHALL SAY GOOD NIGHT TILL IT BE MORROW.

FAIR IS FOUL, AND FOUL IS FAIR...

BETTER a WITTY FOOL than a FOOLISH WIT

WHAT'S in a NAME? THAT WHICH WE CALL a ROSE, BY ANY OTHER NAME WOULD SMELL AS SWEET.

But this time William did not chase them or try to scoop them up. Instead he thought and imagined and finally whispered, "Please good words, stay with me."

Then, he used the tip of his fine new pen to separate the humble jumble of words into lines and phrases, coaxing them onto the page to stay forever.

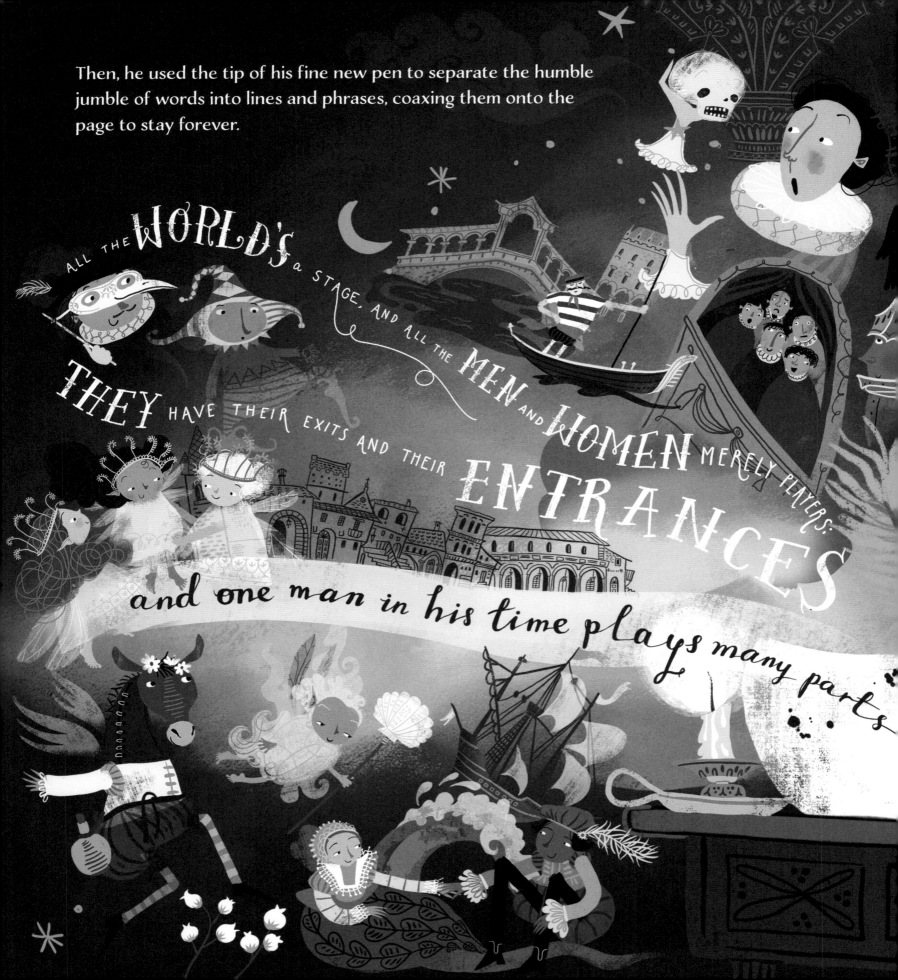

ALL THE WORLD'S a STAGE, AND ALL THE MEN AND WOMEN MERELY PLAYERS: THEY HAVE THEIR EXITS AND THEIR ENTRANCES and one man in his time plays many parts

SOME ARE BORN GREAT, SOME ACHIEVE GREATNESS, AND SOME HAVE GREATNESS THRUST UPON THEM.

Author's Note

While there is a lot we don't know about William Shakespeare's life, this story is loosely inspired by what he might have been like as a child. When the real Shakespeare became a playwright and a poet, he used words with humor and wit and created new words with his vivid imagination.

Some experts credit Shakespeare with creating over 1,000 of our everyday words and phrases. He may have invented these words himself, or may have been the first to take pen to paper and write them down. Either way, even though he lived centuries ago, many of the words he created are still used today. I've used many throughout this story. Can you spot them all?

WILD GOOSE CHASE FAROFF LOVE LETTERS FLIBBERTIGIBBETY madcap
FARMHOUSE BEDROOM ROSE-CHEEKED VANISHED INTO THIN AIR
VAULTING HUMBLE LEAKY JUMBLE GUST HINT GENEROUS ZANY
COLDHEARTED embrace disheartened SCHOOLBOY
GNARLED FASHIONABLE COURTSHIP DOWNSTAIRS USELESS
LONELY green-eyed EVENTFUL GLOOMY WHAT'S DONE IS DONE WELL-BEHAVED

William's Real Words

What about the words that William chases? Those phrases are all quotes from some of Shakespeare's plays:

"This above all . . ."
–Polonius in *Hamlet* (Act 1, Scene 3, line 84)

"My words fly up . . ."
–Claudius in *Hamlet* (Act 3, Scene 3, lines 102–3)

"Boldness, be my friend!"
–Iachimo in *Cymbeline* (Act 1, Scene 6, line 21)

"What's in a name? . . ."
–Juliet in *Romeo and Juliet* (Act 2, Scene 2, lines 46–47)

"Parting is such sweet sorrow . . ."
–Juliet in *Romeo and Juliet* (Act 2, Scene 2, lines 199–201)

"Tis true. The wheel . . ."
–Edmund in *King Lear* (Act 5, Scene 3, lines 208–9)

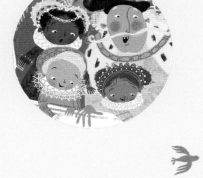

"O, brave new world . . ."
–Miranda in *The Tempest* (Act 5, Scene 1, lines 217–18)

"Better a witty fool . . ."
–Feste in *Twelfth Night* (Act 1, Scene 5, line 34)

"And turn his merry note . . ."
–Amiens in *As You Like It* (Act 2, Scene 5, lines 3–5)

"Fair is foul and foul is fair . . ."
–The Three Witches in *Macbeth* (Act 1, Scene 1, lines 12–13)

"Something wicked this way comes."
–Second Witch in *Macbeth* (Act 4, Scene 1, line 45)

"Tybalt, you rat-catcher . . ."
–Mercutio in *Romeo and Juliet* (Act 3, Scene 1, line 76)

"To be, or not to be . . ."
–Hamlet in *Hamlet* (Act 3, Scene 1, line 64)

"All the world's a stage . . ."
–Jaques in *As You Like It* (Act 2, Scene 7, lines 146–49)

"Some are born great . . ."
–Malvolio in *Twelfth Night* (Act 2, Scene 5, lines 149–50)

Bibliography

Crystal, David, and Ben Crystal. *Shakespeare's Words: A Glossary and Language Companion.* London: Penguin Books, 2002.

Lewis, Luke. "40 Words You Can Trace Back to William Shakespeare." Buzzfeed. Last modified April 23, 2013. https://www.buzzfeed.com/lukelewis/words-you-didnt-realise-william-shakespeare-invented

Mabillard, Amanda. "Words Shakespeare Invented." Shakespeare Online. Last modified August 20, 2000. http://www.shakespeare-online.com/biography/wordsinvented.html

Panganiba, Roma. "20 Words We Owe to Shakspeare." Mental Floss. Last modified January 31, 2013. https://mentalfloss.com/article/48657/20-words-we-owe-williamshakespeare

Schmidt, Alexander. *Shakespeare Lexicon and Quotation Dictionary: A Complete Dictionary of All the English Words, Phrases and Constructions in the Works of the Poet, Volume 1.* England: Dover Publications, 1971.

Shakespeare's Plays from Folger Digital Texts, ed. Barbara Mowat, Paul Werstine, Michael Poston, and Rebecca Niles. Folger Shakespeare Library. www.folgerdigitaltexts.org

Sutcliffe, Jane. *Will's Words: How William Shakespeare Changed the Way You Talk.* Watertown, MA: Charlesbridge Publishing, 2016.

Text copyright © 2020 Donna Guthrie. Illustrations copyright © 2020 Åsa Gilland. First published in 2020 by Page Street Kids, an imprint of Page Street Publishing Co., 27 Congress Street, Suite 105, Salem, MA 01970, www.pagestreetpublishing.com. All rights reserved. No part of this book may be reproduced or used, in any form or by any means, electronic or mechanical, without prior permission in writing from the publisher. Distributed by Macmillan, sales in Canada by The Canadian Manda Group. ISBN-13: 978-1-64567-062-9. ISBN-10: 1-64567-062-7. CIP data for this book is available from the Library of Congress. This book was typeset in Adorn Roman. The illustrations were created digitally with hand-drawn textures. Printed and bound in Shenzhen, Guangdong, China.
20 21 22 23 24 CCO 5 4 3 2

Page Street Publishing uses only materials from suppliers who are committed to responsible and sustainable forest management. Page Street Publishing protects our planet by donating to nonprofits like The Trustees, which focuses on local land conservation.

trustees